The
Tiara
Club
at Silver
Towers

For Princess Elise,
her lovely mum
and her gorgeous grandma too.
VF

For Nila
and the lovely Princess Lili
x SG

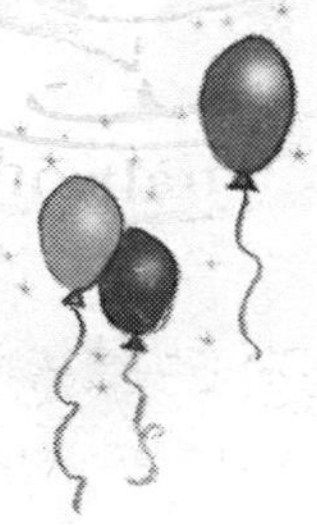

www.tiaraclub.co.uk

ORCHARD BOOKS
338 Euston Road, London NW1 3BH
Orchard Books Australia
Hachette Children's Books
Level 17/207 Kent St, Sydney NSW 2000

A Paperback Original

First published in Great Britain in 2006

A CIP catalogue record for this book is available from the British Library.

ISBN 1 84616 197 5

1 3 5 7 9 10 8 6 4 2

Princess Daisy and the Magical Merry-Go-Round

By Vivian French

Illustrated by Sarah Gibb

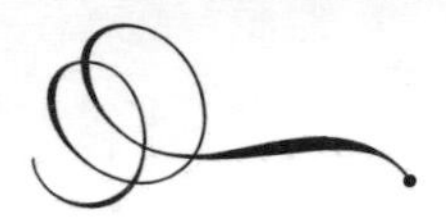

The Royal Palace Academy for the Preparation of Perfect Princesses

(Known to our students as "*The Princess Academy*")

OUR SCHOOL MOTTO:

A Perfect Princess always thinks of others before herself, and is kind, caring and truthful.

Silver Towers offers a complete education for Tiara Club princesses with emphasis on selected outings. The curriculum includes:

Fans and Curtseys

Problem Prime Ministers

A visit to Witch Windlespin

(Royal herbalist, healer and maker of magic potions)

A visit to the Museum of Royal Life

(Students will be well protected from the Poisoned Apple)

Our headteacher, Queen Samantha Joy, is present at all times, and students are well looked after by the school Fairy Godmother, Fairy Angora.

Our resident staff and visiting experts include:

LADY ALBINA MACSPLINTER
(School Secretary)

QUEEN MOTHER MATILDA
(Etiquette, Posture and Poise)

CROWN PRINCE DANDINO
(School Excursions)

FAIRY G
(Head Fairy Godmother)

We award tiara points to encourage our Tiara Club princesses towards the next level. All princesses who win enough points at Silver Towers will attend the Silver Ball, where they will be presented with their Silver Sashes.

Silver Sash Tiara Club princesses are invited to return to Ruby Mansions, our exclusive residence for Perfect Princesses, where they may continue their education at a higher level.

PLEASE NOTE:
Princesses are expected to arrive at the Academy with a *minimum* of:

TWENTY BALL GOWNS
(with all necessary hoops, petticoats, etc)

TWELVE DAY DRESSES

SEVEN GOWNS
suitable for garden parties, and other special day occasions

TWELVE TIARAS

DANCING SHOES
five pairs

VELVET SLIPPERS
three pairs

RIDING BOOTS
two pairs

Cloaks, muffs, stoles, gloves and other essential accessories as required

Hello! I'm Daisy. Princess Daisy.
And I do hope you're enjoying being
at Silver Towers with us. You're exactly
the right kind of princess, you
know – just like my lovely friends,
Charlotte, Katie, Alice, Sophia and Emily.
And not at all like Diamonde and
Gruella – they're SO big-headed.
Do you get nervous before you do
something new? I do – I try SO hard
not to, but I can't help it. And learning
to be a Perfect Princess means
we're ALWAYS doing new things,
or going to new places...

Chapter One

We were sitting in the Homework Room when Princess Freya came ZOOMING in.

"Have any of you seen the noticeboard?" she gasped. "There's a garden fair on Saturday, and a Flower Petal Ball afterwards! Can't stop – got to tell everyone – byeee!" and she was gone.

We stared at each other for a moment, and then Charlotte snatched up her books.

"Quick!" she said. "Let's go and have a look!" The noticeboard is outside the breakfast hall, and if there are any school events or invitations Lady Albina pins them up. We're expected to check the board regularly – but we aren't always very good at remembering!

Anyway, we hurtled down the stairs, but we weren't the first there – LOADS of princesses were staring at the HUGE invitation pinned to the board.

YOU ARE ALL INVITED
TO KING PERCIVAL'S
ROYAL GARDEN FAIR!

This Saturday.

3.00pm until late.

Listen to the Royal Brass Band!

Wander in the flower gardens!

Row on the lake!

Ride on the Marvellous Merry-Go-Round!

NB The day will end with
a Flower Petal Ball

"Wow!" said Charlotte. "That sounds SO brilliant! And it's Saturday tomorrow!"

Alice's eyes were shining. "I ADORE merry-go-rounds," she said. "Let's all have a go together, and we can whirl round and round and ROUND!"

"YES!" Emily and Katie sounded just as thrilled as Alice.

"Merry-go-rounds are the BEST!" Sophia said. "What do you think, Daisy?"

"Yes," I said, "it'll be fun." And I hoped I sounded as if I really truly meant it.

Does that sound odd? The trouble was, I'd been secretly hoping we wouldn't have another trip out for a little while. We'd been to King Percival's before, so I knew that bit would be all right – but I wasn't at all sure if I liked the idea of a merry-go-round. I'd never been on one, and I was certain I'd do something silly, like getting dizzy and falling off. For a moment I wondered if I could pretend to be ill the next day – but then I remembered I was trying to be a Perfect Princess, and earn enough tiara points to win my Silver Sash, and a place at Ruby Mansions.

"Perfect Princesses," I told myself firmly, "don't tell lies! And they try to be BRAVE!"

Sophia was still looking at the invitation on the board.

"It doesn't tell us what to wear," she said. "Do we have to dress as flowers for a Flower Petal Ball?"

Princess Diamonde and her twin sister, Gruella, heard her, and Diamonde sniggered.

"Sophia could go as a dandelion, couldn't she, Gruella?"

"ALL the Silver Rose Roomers could go as weeds!" Gruella said, and the two of them collapsed in a fit of giggles.

Sophia TOTALLY ignored them, and took my arm. "Shall we go and ask Fairy Angora?"

I nodded. Fairy Angora is the fairy godmother at Silver Towers, and she was sure to know.

"FANCY! Sophia's actually had a good idea!" Diamonde said loudly. "Gruella – why don't we see Fairy Angora at break time?" And she flounced away.

"Quick!" Katie said. "Let's go right now!"

The six of us hurried along the corridor, and knocked at Fairy Angora's door.

"DO come in!" Fairy Angora has the loveliest tinkling voice. "Door – OPEN!"

The door turned a glowing pink, but it stayed shut. Sometimes Fairy Angora's magic just doesn't work.

Alice grinned and turned the handle, and we trooped inside.

Fairy Angora was sitting at her desk, which had a vase of gorgeous apple blossom on it.

"What can I do for you, my darlings?" she asked.

"Please," Sophia said, "we're not sure what to wear tomorrow."

"Wear your prettiest summer dresses, angels!" Fairy Angora said. "Something fresh and flowery – that'll be perfect for the fair AND the Flower Petal Ball."

We looked at each other anxiously. NONE of us had flowery dresses.

"Don't worry, darlings!" Fairy Angora had seen our faces. "Pop in here after lessons with what you've got." She waved at her vase. "I've been practising a little flowery magic, so we'll see what I can do! But don't be late, my angels. I've got a meeting with King Percival, and I mustn't keep him waiting!"

Chapter Two

Of course we felt MUCH better after seeing Fairy Angora. In fact, we didn't really concentrate all that day because we were so busy wondering what our dresses would look like...which wasn't a good idea at all.

Queen Mother Matilda gave us two minus points each for

whispering during our lesson in the Gracious Acceptance of Royal Bouquets, and then Crown Prince Dandino told me off for not paying attention when he was showing us how to Step out of a Coach with Dignity and Poise.

"You must stay in for an extra half an hour after classes," he ordered, "and PRACTISE!"

I BEGGED him to let me go, but he wouldn't change his mind. Emily and Sophia pleaded with him too, and then he said we ALL had to stay...it was AWFUL!

As soon as he let us go we DASHED up to Silver Rose Room to collect our dresses, and then ZOOMED down to Fairy Angora's room. We lined up outside her door – and that's where Lady Albina saw us.

"May I ask exactly what you girls are doing?" she asked. She never sounds very friendly. Alice says her big sister reckons Lady Albina doesn't like anybody except Queen Samantha Joy.

"Please," Katie said, "we're here to see Fairy Angora."

"Well, you won't find her HERE," Lady Albina snapped. "She's having a very important meeting with King Percival, and she won't be free until the garden fair tomorrow."

As Lady Albina swept away we looked at each other blankly.

"No flowery dresses," Sophia said, and she sounded SO sad.

I felt COMPLETELY terrible. If ONLY I'd paid attention during Prince Dandino's lesson we'd have been in time to catch Fairy Angora.

Emily knew what I was thinking, and squeezed my hand. "At least we'll all be the same," she said. "Think how horrid it would be if half of us had fabulous flowery dresses and the others didn't!"

"That's right!" Alice was pretending to be cheerful. "Who

wants to look like a flowerbed, anyway?"

"YES!" Charlotte actually managed a smile. "Let's be different!"

I didn't say anything. I was trying hard not to cry.

*

We did our best to look summery for the Garden Fair. Alice and Katie both had gingham check dresses, and Sophia's was white with a little pink stripe.

Emily's dress had blue spots, and Charlotte and I were both wearing pink.

They were pretty dresses, but when we saw what the other princesses were wearing we did feel VERY ordinary.

"OOOOOH!" Diamonde trilled when she saw us. "It's the WEEDS!" She twirled round so we could see the lovely twirls of honeysuckle on her rustling silk skirts.

"OUR mother ALWAYS makes sure we have dresses for EVERY occasion!" Gruella told us, and she and Diamonde smirked at each other.

Gruella's dress was sprinkled with the sweetest little primroses, and there were more primroses on her tiara. I couldn't help thinking that even though she's not always very nice, she did look GORGEOUS.

"Everybody ready?" Crown Prince Dandino was waiting at

the door. "Hop in the coaches, and we'll be off!"

We hung back a little as the coaches filled with chattering princesses.

"We can still have fun," Emily said bravely.

"That's right." Sophia suddenly sat up, and smiled. "I'm sure Perfect Princesses don't mind WHAT they wear!"

"Of course they don't," Katie said firmly.

"Diamonde will have to be REALLY careful of her dress," Charlotte pointed out. "She was tripping over it just getting into the coach!"

Alice grinned. "Let's go on the merry-go-round as soon as we get there! Agreed?"

Everyone shouted "YES!"...and I did too, although I had a wobbly feeling in my stomach.

Just in case anyone noticed, I said, "Is it all right if we go for a boat ride on the lake straight afterwards? I LOVE boats!"

"Fine by me!" Alice said cheerfully, but I saw Sophia and Emily look at each other.

"What's wrong?" I asked.

"Erm..." Emily said, and she was blushing. "I'm really REALLY sorry – but I don't like the water very much. I'm HOPELESS at swimming!"

"It's HORRID being scared of things," Sophia said. "You mustn't worry, Emily – I'm always terrified if I think I can't put my feet on the bottom!"

Chapter Three

I looked at my friends, and felt SO much better...but I also felt a little bit mean. They'd been brave enough to say they were scared, and I hadn't.

"Actually," I said, "can I tell you something?"

They looked at me in surprise.

"Can't you swim either, Daisy?"

asked Katie.

"It's not that," I said, "it's the merry-go-round. It makes my legs go wobbly every time I think about it!"

There was a second's silence, and then we all began to laugh. It was as if a HUGE weight had fallen off me, and I think Emily and Sophia felt a little bit the same.

"Right!" Alice said. "We'll ALL look after each other! First we'll try the merry-go-round, and then the boating lake – and if anyone wants to sit and watch that's TOTALLY OK!"

And we solemnly shook hands.

We were much the last to arrive at King Percival's palace. The coach we were supposed to travel in had a loose wheel, and we had to wait while Prince Dandino organised another one. It was SO frustrating!

By the time we finally got there we were absolutely BURSTING with excitement, even if we weren't wearing flowery dresses. We totally tumbled out of the coach (it was a good thing Prince Dandino didn't see us!) and stared round.

King Percival's gardens looked BEAUTIFUL. Silver balloons were tied on every bush and tree, and they looked SO pretty as they shone in the sunshine! But the princesses and princes and queens and kings who were wandering around didn't look as if they were having a particularly wonderful time. We saw Princess Lisa and Princess Jemima, and they were sitting at the edge of the lake looking so BORED!

"What's the matter?" I asked. "Aren't you having fun?"

Princess Lisa shook her head. "There's nothing much to do. The brass band hasn't turned up, the merry-go-round isn't working properly, and there are only two boats on the lake, and Princess Eglantine and Princess Nancy have been hogging them for AGES! We're just hanging about waiting for the Flower Petal Ball."

"Oh dear," I said, but Alice pulled at my arm.

"I can see the merry-go-round!" she said, her eyes sparkling. "Let's have a look at it!"

Emily held one of my hands as we walked across the grass, and Sophia the other. As we got closer, I could see the merry-go-round did look AMAZING.

It had the prettiest little coaches and carriages pulled by the sweetest silver ponies – and there, standing right in front of it, was Fairy Angora. She was deep in conversation with King Percival, who was looking very gloomy.

"Maybe we could ask her about our dresses!" Sophia whispered.

"She looks too busy at the moment," Alice said. "Why don't we try to have a go on the merry-go-round?"

"DO let's!" Emily said. 'Daisy can share with me, and then she'll be fine! OK, Daisy?"

I nodded, and I was just stepping into a sweet little carriage when Diamonde and Gruella appeared.

"Oh!" Gruella almost smiled. "That looks FUN!" She climbed in and sat beside me before I could say anything.

Diamonde frowned. "Gruella! Merry-go-rounds are for babies!" she sniffed, but she pushed me to one side so she could squash in too.

Emily made a sympathetic face at me, and sat down in the carriage next to mine. "Will you be all right?" she asked.

"OOOOH! Is poor little Daisy scared?" Diamonde asked.

I smoothed my skirts, and tried to look calm. "I'm QUITE all right," I said – and I SO hoped it was true!

The merry-go-round began to turn, but it went SO slowly. I kept thinking it was about to speed up, but it didn't. It lurched and shuddered as if it was about to stop any second, and it squeaked terribly.

King Percival and Fairy Angora looked up just as my carriage drew level with them.

"Oh NO!" King Percival groaned. "Still going slow, what? TYPICAL!"

"Everything's going wrong." He glared at Fairy Angora. "That's the trouble with magic! You can't rely on it! I'm going to find the Royal Engineer!" He stamped away across the grass.

Fairy Angora was looking very flustered. "POOR King Percival," she said. "Even the Royal Brass Band hasn't arrived yet."

"Couldn't you use your wand to

make things better?" I asked.

Fairy Angora hesitated. "I have been helping, my angel," she said. "I was here yesterday for AGES, sorting things out." She sighed. "Sometimes I think my magic isn't very good."

I felt SO sorry for her. "It wouldn't take much magic to make the merry-go-round work, would it?"

Diamonde sat back, folded her arms and sneered. "Silly Daisy! She means she CAN'T make it work!"

Chapter Four

I was so shocked! I couldn't believe she'd been so rude. Fairy Angora went BRIGHT PINK, and looked really angry.

"Princess Diamonde," she said, "take TEN minus tiara points, and come and see me in my office tomorrow!" She tapped our silver pony on its nose. "And for your information, young lady, I certainly CAN make this merry-go-round work!"

There was a flash, a shower of stars...and our silver pony neighed, shook its head, and charged off the merry-go-round

with our carriage rattling behind it – and at once all the other ponies followed!

I hung on tightly as we bumped and bounced over the grass. Diamonde and Gruella screamed and screamed and SCREAMED.

On either side princesses shrieked and ran, and I could see Lady Albina staring at us with her mouth wide open.

The ponies swerved round a flowerbed, and dashed straight

for the lake. They zoomed up to the edge, and hurled themselves in. As they swam out towards the middle of the lake, there was a shower of silver stars – and they VANISHED!

It was SO strange. Suddenly, we were floating peacefully on the water. Diamonde was still screaming, and Gruella was wailing that they were going to be drowned, but it really did feel safe.

I could see crowds gathering at the edge of the lake, and poor King Percival wiping his forehead and trying to calm everyone down, but I didn't feel scared at all. But then I remembered Emily and Sophia, and I turned to look at them. Their coaches were floating behind mine, and they were smiling at me, although I did think they looked rather pale.

Alice and Katie and Charlotte were grinning from ear to ear, so I knew they were fine. I peered out of our carriage, and it rocked wildly. Diamonde and Gruella screeched, but I didn't take any notice. The water was very clear and clean, and it didn't look deep.

In fact, it didn't look very deep at all...

I took my shoes off.

"Daisy's going to leave us here to DROOOOOOOOWN!" Gruella moaned.

"Oh no! I want MUMMY!" Diamonde howled.

I stepped out of the carriage, and the water only just reached the hem of my dress. "Come on," I said to Gruella and Diamonde. "I'll hold your hands."

As we all reached the shore there was a loud cheer, and King Percival stepped forward to help us onto the bank.

"Well done, young Daisy," he said. "Sorry about that. Was almost sure something would go wrong. Shouldn't have tried to mess with magic, I—"

But at that moment Queen Samantha Joy came sailing through the crowd, with Fairy Angora close behind her.

"I THINK," Queen Samantha Joy said, and her voice was shaking because she was so angry, "we need a very good EXPLANATION, King Percival! There seems to be something EXTREMELY unusual about your merry-go-round!"

If it hadn't been so awful, it would have been funny. King Percival looked like a naughty boy who'd been caught stealing apples. He hung his head, and shuffled his feet – and that was when I stepped forward.

Chapter Five

"Excuse me, Your Majesty, I said, and I curtsied as low as I could, "it's not King Percival's fault. It was me—" I stopped to swallow hard. 'You see, I suggested that Fairy Angora used magic on the merry-go-round. I'm TRULY sorry—" but I had to stop.

Fairy Angora was waving her

wand at me. "It wasn't Princess Daisy's fault at all," she said. "It was MINE—"

"HARRUMPH!" King Percival made the LOUDEST snorting noise. "Nothing of the kind! ALL my fault! Wanted to have a good day, d'you see – persuaded Fairy Angora to do me a favour. Had her making magic all yesterday, you see – got her to turn my carriage ponies into merry-go-round ponies. Stupid, really. Should have known I'd mess up. Humble apologies, Your Majesty. Won't happen again!"

"I see." Queen Samantha Joy's

voice was shaking so much I couldn't help staring at her – and now she seemed to be LAUGHING! "Well, King Percival, I have to tell you that I usually find garden fairs a touch on the boring side – but I shall ALWAYS remember this one!"

"But WE didn't think it was funny!" Diamonde said, glaring.

"That's right!" Gruella said. "We nearly DROWNED!"

Fairy Angora whispered something to Queen Samantha

Joy. Our headteacher looked at Diamonde, and she was suddenly VERY serious.

"If I am correct, Princess Diamonde, it was YOU that made Fairy Angora so angry she forgot to behave in a suitably responsible manner. There is a coach waiting at the entrance to the garden, and I suggest you and your sister go STRAIGHT back to Silver Towers to think about your attitude. The rest of us will continue enjoying the fair. King Percival, do I hear your brass band? They must have arrived after all!"

Queen Samantha Joy tucked her arm into King Percival's, and walked him away. She had almost disappeared into the crowd when she turned, and called, "Fairy Angora! DO see those poor girls don't catch their death of cold!"

Fairy Angora was standing staring at the lake, a puzzled look on her face. When she heard Queen Samantha Joy, she jumped.

"Oh! You poor little darlings!" She looked at our damp dresses. "Oh oh OH! I remember now. You were going to come and see me yesterday about your dresses, but I had to rush off and meet King

Percival! Oh, I'm so very VERY sorry! What a TERRIBLE time you've had." She pulled her wand out of her bag, and blew on the end of it. "Now...let me see...can I get this right, do you think?"

She twirled her wand in the air – and we GASPED. Our dresses were totally AMAZING! It was as if they'd been made from a froth of pink and white apple blossom, with shimmery pink petticoats. They were the most GORGEOUS dresses I'd ever seen – and we had glittery pink shoes to match!

"THANK YOU!" we chorused. "Thank you VERY MUCH!"

Fairy Angora beamed. "They have turned out well, haven't they?" she said.

"Now, if I could only work out what happened to those ponies..."

"LOOK!" It was Katie, and she was pointing at the lake. "THERE they are! They're trotting out of the water...and they're not even wet!" She rubbed her eyes. "But they're not silver any more. They're REAL!"

"Of course they are," Fairy Angora said, sounding very relieved. "And I'm SO pleased to see them! I couldn't think WHAT I was going to say to King Percival if they'd really gone for good. Now, are you going to help

me catch them? Maybe you'd like to ride them across to the crystal tower. It must almost be time for the Flower Petal Ball!"

Of course we were thrilled...and as we rode round the palace ground and up to the crystal tower we felt like the most Perfect Princesses in the whole wide world.

Chapter Six

Have you ever been to a Flower Petal Ball? It was SO magic. You couldn't see the walls for the garlands of flowers, and as we danced, petals drifted in the air. The scent of roses and lavender and honeysuckle was everywhere, and beautiful butterflies fluttered from blossom to blossom.

As the evening grew darker, silver stars floated up into the velvet night sky, and tiny twinkly lights shone in among the glossy ivy leaves that twisted round the tall stone pillars.

King Percival's Royal Orchestra played the SWEETEST music, and we danced until our feet were sore...and our gorgeous apple blossom dresses glimmered and shimmered in the twilight. It was absolutely HEAVENLY.

*

When we finally rolled home to Silver Towers I was SO tired. We hung our gorgeous dresses up, and whispered "Good night!" to each other as we crawled into bed.

"Thank you for a LOVELY time, Daisy," Emily said sleepily.

"Me?" I said, surprised. "I didn't do anything!"

"Yes you did." Katie yawned a huge yawn. "You made it a FUN day!"

"I didn't exactly mean to," I said. "Anyway, it was fun because we were there together..."

And I meant it. Friends are the best thing ever...and I'm SO glad you're our friend too.

What happens next?

Find out in

and the Crystal Slipper

Hi! How are you doing? It's so brilliant that you're here at Silver Towers - you're a real STAR. Not like the twins - Princess Diamonde and Princess Gruella. They're SO stuck-up and horrible. Sometimes I almost hope they won't get enough tiara points to win their Silver Sashes and go on to Ruby Mansions...but that's NOT the way a Perfect Princess ought to think!

Oh - I forgot to say. I'm Princess Alice and I share the Silver Rose Room with Charlotte, Katie, Daisy, Sophia and Emily. They're my best friends, and we try to do everything together...

Check out

website at:

www.tiaraclub.co.uk

You'll find Perfect Princess games and fun things to do, as well as news on the Tiara Club and all your favourite princesses!

Win a Tiara Club *Perfect Princess Prize!*

Look for the secret word in mirror writing hidden in a tiara in each of the Tiara Club books. Each book has one word. Put together the six words from books 7 to 12 to make a special Perfect Princess sentence, then send it to us together with 20 words or more on why you like the Tiara Club books. Each month, we will put the correct entries in a draw and one lucky reader will receive a magical Perfect Princess prize!

Send your Perfect Princess sentence, your name and your address on a postcard to:
THE TIARA CLUB COMPETITION,
Orchard Books, 338 Euston Road,
London, NW1 3BH

Australian readers should write to:
Hachette Children's Books,
Level 17/207 Kent Street, Sydney, NSW 2000.

Only one entry per child.
Final draw: 31 August 2007

By Vivian French
Illustrated by Sarah Gibb

PRINCESS CHARLOTTE AND THE BIRTHDAY BALL	ISBN	1 84362 863 5
PRINCESS KATIE AND THE SILVER PONY	ISBN	1 84362 860 0
PRINCESS DAISY AND THE DAZZLING DRAGON	ISBN	1 84362 864 3
PRINCESS ALICE AND THE MAGICAL MIRROR	ISBN	1 84362 861 9
PRINCESS SOPHIA AND THE SPARKLING SURPRISE	ISBN	1 84362 862 7
PRINCESS EMILY AND THE BEAUTIFUL FAIRY	ISBN	1 84362 859 7

The Tiara Club at Silver Towers

PRINCESS CHARLOTTE AND THE ENCHANTED ROSE	ISBN	1 84616 195 9
PRINCESS KATIE AND THE DANCING BROOM	ISBN	1 84616 196 7
PRINCESS DAISY AND THE MAGICAL MERRY-GO-ROUND	ISBN	1 84616 197 5
PRINCESS ALICE AND THE CRYSTAL SLIPPER	ISBN	1 84616 198 3
PRINCESS SOPHIA AND THE PRINCE'S PARTY	ISBN	1 84616 199 1
PRINCESS EMILY AND THE WISHING STAR	ISBN	1 84616 200 9

All priced at £3.99.